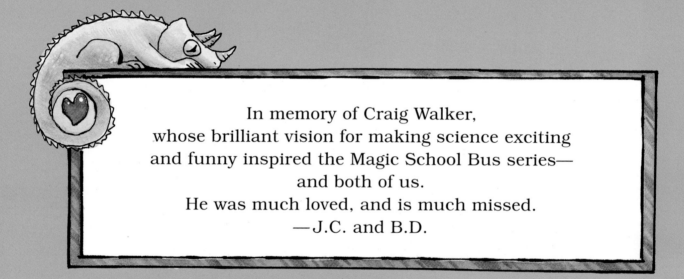

In memory of Craig Walker,
whose brilliant vision for making science exciting
and funny inspired the Magic School Bus series—
and both of us.
He was much loved, and is much missed.
—J.C. and B.D.

The Magic School Bus

and the Climate Challenge

Scenery
for the
Class Play...

WHITE

The Magic School Bus

and the Climate Challenge

By Joanna Cole

Illustrated by Bruce Degen

RECYCLED PAPER

Scholastic Press / New York

Many have helped in the making of this book. In particular, our sincere thanks go to

Dr. Bill Chameides, Dean and Nicholas Professor of the Environment, Duke University,

for his enthusiastic and informed review.

Library of Congress Cataloging-in-Publication Data is available

ISBN: 978-0-590-10826-3

Text copyright © 2010 by Joanna Cole.
Illustrations copyright © 2010 by Bruce Degen.
All rights reserved. Published by Scholastic Press,
an imprint of Scholastic Inc., *Publishers since 1920.*
THE MAGIC SCHOOL BUS, SCHOLASTIC, SCHOLASTIC PRESS, and associated
logos are trademarks and/or registered trademarks of Scholastic Inc.

10 9 8 7 6 5 4 3 2 1   10 11 12 13 14 15
Printed in China
First edition, March 2010

The text type was set in 15-point Bookman Light.
The illustrator used pen and ink, watercolor, color pencil, and gouache for the paintings in this book.
The text of this book prints on 100% recovered fiber of which 50% is post-consumer waste.

To all our friends in Korea.
We will never forget your warm and enthusiastic
welcome to The Magic School Bus, and to us.
— J.C. and B.D.

For example, take the day we started to study global warming. We were going to put on a play about Earth and all the changes that are happening.

The Friz had brought a book from home, and we were using the pictures to help us paint the scenery.

WHAT IS GLOBAL WARMING?
by Carlos

Global warming is a rise in the average temperature of the land and water on Earth. Today, the average temperature is more than 1 degree F warmer than it was 100 years ago.

One degree doesn't sound like much, but one small degree has caused big changes already— ice melting, seas rising, and more freak weather!

"Ms. Frizzle's book is kind of old," said Tim. "It came out before things really started heating up." "I'll go online to get new pictures," said Wanda. She headed for a computer, but Ms. Frizzle was already out the door. "Come on, class," she called. "Bring my book, please."

Before you could say "North Pole,"
the Friz herded us onto the bus.
She pushed a few buttons and pulled a few levers.
Then we were on our way to the Arctic Sea—
a place with a completely different climate.

When we got there, Dorothy Ann opened
Ms. Frizzle's old book.
The pictures showed ice everywhere.
There was still plenty of ice in the Arctic,
but a lot had melted, and more
was melting all the time.

MELTING CAUSES
MORE MELTING
by Tim

Ice is white. White reflects most of the sunlight that hits it. So the sun can't heat up the ice.
Water is not white. It absorbs most of the sunlight that hits it. So the water gets warmer.

SUN

ICE REFLECTS

WATER ABSORBS

This starts a dangerous loop:
- The warm water melts more ice.
- That means there is more water.
- This water takes in more sunlight.
- So the water gets warmer and melts even more ice.
And so on, and so on, until all the ice is gone.

HOW IT LOOKS NOW

IN THE ARCTIC, AN AREA HAS MELTED THAT'S THE SIZE OF TEXAS AND CALIFORNIA COMBINED!

CALIFORNIA

TEXAS

Ms. Frizzle steered the bus-plane
all over the earth.
We saw changes everywhere.

THE ATMOSPHERE ~ IT'S A GAS
by Phoebe

The earth is surrounded by layers of gases. All this gas is called the atmosphere.

I CALL IT AIR!

WHAT ARE GASES?
by Arnold

Gases float and fill up any space they occupy.
A gas is thinner and lighter than a solid or liquid.

ICE	WATER	STEAM
SOLID	LIQUID	GAS

GASES IN THE ATMOSPHERE
by Molly

Most of the atmosphere is made up of these two gases:

OXYGEN (O_2)

NITROGEN (N_2)

"Aren't you children wondering why the earth is getting warmer and warmer?" asked Ms. Frizzle. Actually, we were wondering why she was steering the bus-plane higher and higher.

MS. FRIZZLE, AREN'T THERE NATURAL UPS AND DOWNS IN THE CLIMATE?

YES, BUT THEY DO NOT REALLY EXPLAIN WHAT IS HAPPENING ON THE EARTH TODAY.

YAPTOP

DOES ANYTHING EXPLAIN WHAT HAPPENS IN THIS CLASS?

"Most of today's warming is caused by the increasing level of heat-trapping gases in the atmosphere," said the Friz. "Heat-trapping gases are also called greenhouse gases."
She had that funny gleam in her eye.
We could tell something "interesting" was about to happen.

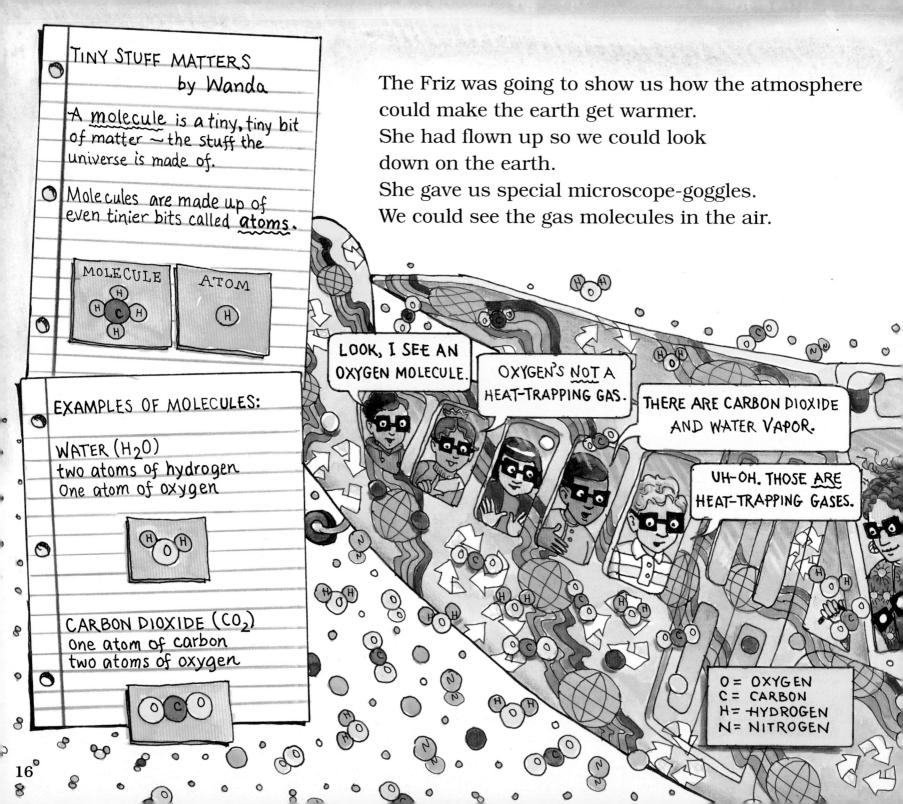

The greenhouse gases trapped some of the heat. That heat headed back to Earth again. It raised the earth's temperature even higher than before.

Our teacher shooed us back on the bus-plane. Like it or not, we were on our way to see some alternative energy.

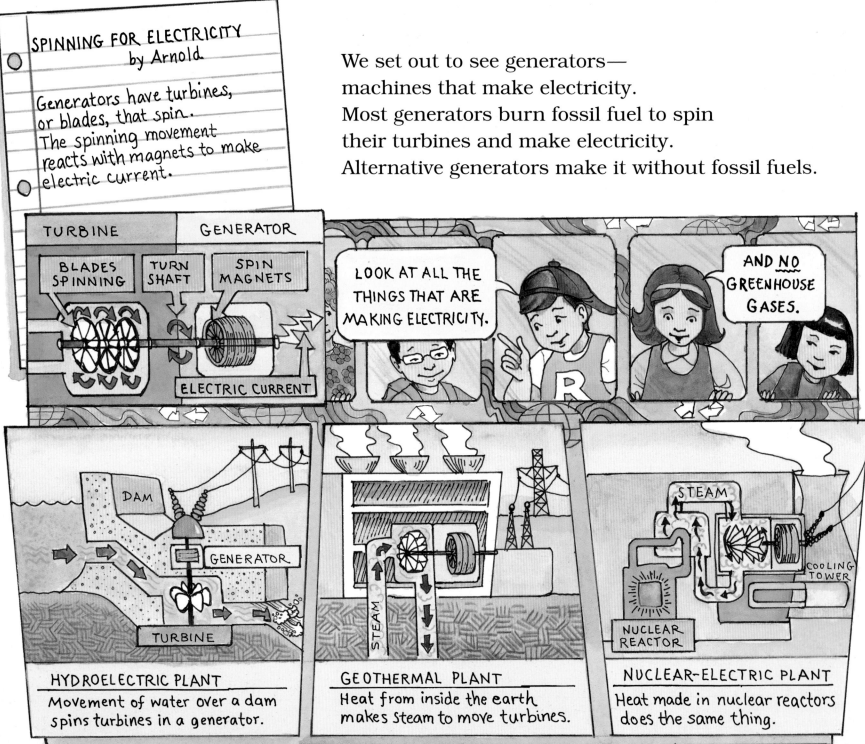

We set out to see generators—
machines that make electricity.
Most generators burn fossil fuel to spin
their turbines and make electricity.
Alternative generators make it without fossil fuels.

In the countryside, we saw
another alternative: windmills.
The wind turned the blades.
"Anything that moves has energy," the Friz said.
"And energy can be made into electricity."

As we flew over a desert, we heard a loud crunch.
Out the window, we saw the bus-plane's wings fall off!
"Ms. Frizzle!" we yelled, but she didn't seem to notice.
She was too busy telling us about more
alternative energy.
This time she pointed to a huge
solar generator below.

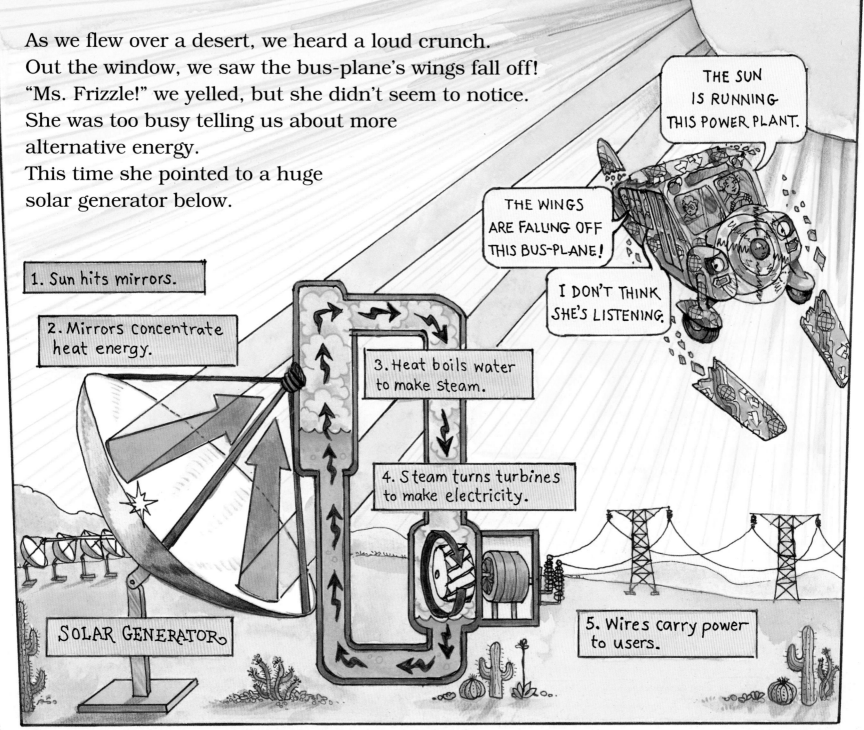

The bus made a crash landing.
Oops, we mean a *splash* landing.
We were floating in a solar-heated swimming pool.
Ms. Frizzle kept talking, telling us about solar cells.
They make energy directly from the sun—
with no moving parts.

SOLAR CELLS:
YOU ARE MY SUNSHINE
by Ralphie

Solar cells are made of special materials that make electric current when light shines on them.

The cells are microscopic. They can be put on panels or on a thin film.

Solar bags charge laptops.

CHILDREN, DO YOU NOTICE THE MANY DEVICES POWERED BY SOLAR CELLS?

ROOF COVERED WITH SOLAR FILM MAKES ALL THE ELECTRICITY A FAMILY NEEDS.

UM...MS. FRIZZLE, DO YOU NOTICE THAT THE BUS IS A GIANT POOL TOY?

WALKERVILLE TOWN POOL

HEY! NO SPLASHING!

LENNY THE LIFEGUARD

Solar panels heat pools...

...and run garden lights.

A solar "briefcase" makes energy wherever you need it.

The bus stopped being a pool toy,
so we rode into town.
Everywhere, people were saving energy.
Instead of driving private cars, many were
using trains, buses, taxis, and bikes, as
well as more fuel-efficient vehicles.

WORKING TOGETHER!
by Wanda

Richer countries can help poorer countries get alternative energy.

That way, less CO_2 will go into the whole earth's atmosphere, and we'll all be better off.

"We're back!" the Friz exclaimed, pulling into the school parking lot. We put our goggles back on, and we saw greenhouse gases all over the place.

WALKERVILLE ELEMENTARY SCHOOL

THIS IS NOT THE ONLY PLACE THERE'S CO_2.

RIGHT! IT'S ALL OVER THE EARTH!

MS. FRIZZLE, HOW CAN WE CHANGE THINGS ALL OVER THE EARTH?

CLASS, WE CAN START RIGHT HERE, RIGHT NOW!

We had to start saving energy right away.
"Conserve, conserve, conserve!" shouted the Friz.
"Recycle, recycle, recycle!"

I CONSERVE PAPER BY WRITING ON THE BACK.

I CONSERVE PAPER, TOO— BY NOT DOING MY HOMEWORK!

USED PAINT JARS

OLD NEWSPAPERS

MORE WORDS FROM D.A.

Conserve means to avoid waste.

Recycle means to treat waste materials so they can be used again.

RECYCLING SAVES ENERGY
by Tim

Making new cans from recycled cans uses 30% less energy than making them from new aluminum.

KIDS CAN...
Recycle cans and bottles!

CANS

BOTTLES

A LITTLE CAN DO A LOT
If your town recycled 2,000 pounds of aluminum cans, it would save enough energy to heat the typical home for 10 years.

We started making changes at our school.
There was plenty of room for improvement.
Then we called the mayor of our town.
Then we wrote to the president.

We told everyone, "Let's cut down on greenhouse gases now!"

- Don't leave the fridge open too long.
- Buy Energy Star appliances.

IT'S NOT COOL TO LEAVE THE FRIDGE OPEN!

ENERGY STAR

- Buy things with less packaging.
- Buying MORE local produce...

...SAVES ON PACKAGING AND TRANSPORTATION.

- Use cloth shopping bags.
- Buy LESS bottled water.

- Air-dry your laundry.

A LITTLE CAN DO A LOT

If every household in the U.S. switched three lights to compact fluorescent lamps (CFLS), it would reduce as much CO_2 as taking 3.5 million cars off the road.

That's because old incandescent bulbs waste a lot of energy making heat. CFLS use most of their energy making light.

THE LESS ENERGY YOU USE, THE LESS CO_2 GOES INTO THE AIR.

Finally, we had time to put on our play.
It was about everything we had seen on our trip.
We showed what global warming was doing to our planet.
And we told about how people can help.

WARMING ISN'T SO GOOD FOR OUR FORESTS, EITHER.

IT CAUSES DROUGHTS AND WILDFIRES...

... AND IT BRINGS MORE INSECT PESTS.

YUM! WE LOVE GLOBAL WARMING!

HEY, BUGS! STOP EATING OUR FORESTS!

MSBTV

APPLAUSE!

Can you believe it?
A TV station found out about us,
and we got to be on television!

QUESTIONS FOR MS. FRIZZLE'S CLASS
... an online chat

Q. Can a class really go up in the sky and ride sunbeams into the earth?
from IvannaNO@once.now

A. According to our research, only Ms. Frizzle's class can do that.
from Dorothy.Ann@a.loss.to.explain.net

Q. Why are you so worried about global warming? There were warm times in Earth's past, weren't there?
from Onceupon@time.now

A. In past times, Earth's climate has been cool, cold, warm, and hot. But these changes have happened over millions of years. Animals and plants had time to adjust. The warming we see now has happened in only a few hundred years. We can't adapt that fast.
from Ralphie@a.gallop.net

Q. Can a single person really change things?
from Juan@atime4change.net

A. One individual can't make a big difference.
But millions of individuals can!
from Phoebe@longlast/together.net

Q. Don't we need bigger help?
from a.giant@least?.net

A. You're right. We need all the governments of the
world to cooperate in solving the climate crisis.
from Ms.Frizzle@the.crossroads

Q. Why does Ms. Frizzle always go on such
weird class trips?
from kids@risk?safety.net

A. That's what I would like to know.
from Arnold@home.sweet.home